WITHDRAWN
UTSA LIBRARIES

WITHDRAWN
UTSA LIBRARIES

LITHOGRAPHY
WITHDRAWN

deep-tap tree

THE UNIVERSITY OF MASSACHUSETTS PRESS   AMHERST 1978

ALEXANDER HUTCHISON

deep-tap tree

Acknowledgment is due to the editors of the following where
some of these pieces appeared for the first time.
"Climacteric," *Stand* 16:1, 1974.
"Lyke-wake," *Prism International* 14:1, 1974.
"Reticulum," *Ambit 61, 1975.*
"To Freyja," *Prism International* 16:2, 1977.
"Riguarda," "In Fire the Voice Goes Further," *The Malahat
Review* 45, 1978.
"Princess Palestrina" and "Interrogations for the Justiciary"
were recorded by *DNA* for Radio Canada International,
Transcriptions Series: E-1057, 1972.
"At the Breaking of the Stag," "Of Akbar," "The Sooth of
Birds" and "The Death of Odinn" were published as broadsides
in collaboration with Will Carter of the Rampant Lions
Press, Cambridge, in 1977.

Copyright © 1978 by Alexander Hutchison   All rights reserved
Library of Congress Catalog Card Number 78-53174
ISBN 0-87023-251-4 (cloth); 0-87023-255-x (paper)
Printed in the United States of America
Designed by Mary Mendell
Library of Congress Cataloging in Publication Data appear on
the last page of the book.

L   RY
The University of Texas
At San Antonio

'he is called the heron of oblivion'

Contents

Impresa   *1*

To Freyja   *3*

1

Climacteric   7

Mr. Scales Walks His Dog   *8*

In Brass and in Brimstone I Burn like a Bell   *10*

2

The Shrug, the Hum, or Ha   *15*

Princess Palestrina   *16*

Undertow   *17*

Political Digression   *18*

Interrogations for the Justiciary   *19*

Reticulum   *21*

The Rumly Go   *26*

Construct by Simple Succession   *27*

3

Lyke-wake   *31*

4

Receipt *37*

Remorse *38*

Poem Beginning with Love as a Waterfall *39*

5

Link-light *43*

The Dead-*Carn* Shifting Slowly in the Drift *44*

A Slate Rubbed Smooth *45*

Traces *46*

6

Riguarda *49*

In Fire the Voice Goes Further *51*

7

At the Breaking of the Stag *57*

Of Akbar *58*

The Sooth of Birds *59*

The Death of Odinn *60*

Notes *63*

deep-tap tree

Impresa

Iron on iron: and so we sharpen
each other's countenance;

Skin to skin: so we kindle
each day's heart.

To Freyja

I
Lady of linen cloth
blue flax flower

give me the girdle of a languid beast

II
Bone fitted   sinew fitted
tongue to tongue-tip

III
Fire-slit rider of the golden pool
and bristled field

here is my chastity sold to dwarfs
for a necklace of garnet

IV
Straddled-in-blood
keep me from the wounds of distance

1

Climacteric

This time something threatens to give way entirely:
Ridgepole, roofbeam, whatever you imagine as lasting
This time will fail to remember words that fell so bright
And fast about we found no shelter but the storm itself.

Burning branches in stoves and stalls, juniper burning
And the place thick with the smell of it. Star-bane;
Lesion in the thew of space.

Even the confidence of God at knell of the hardest season
Withers and rots away.

These purposes splinter in a rented room;
Intention, surface, prospect before, behind
Is all some thriftless illusion
Drawn down in a trough of queer air.

I can guess at it—tailing, diminished,
Acknowledge a thread of worn profit,
Even an infection slowly taken—

Nature scourged by sequent effects:
No lamp of bronze, no drum
At the cross-tree—
                    Appetite
And intelligence and little else;
Blood loop on a dry beaten run.

Mr. Scales Walks His Dog

The dog is so old dust flies out from its arse as it runs;
the dog is so old its tongue rattles in its mouth, its eyes were changed
in the 17th century, its legs are borrowed from a Louis Fourteen bedside
cabinet.
The dog is barking with an antique excitement.
Scales dog is so old its barks hang in the air like old socks,
like faded paper flowers.
It is so old it played the doorman of the Atlantic Hotel in *The Last Laugh*,
so old it played the washroom attendant too.
Scales dog is so old he never learned to grow old gracefully.
Scales dog bites in stages.
Scales dog smells of naphtha.
Scales dog misjudges steps and trips.
Scales dog begs for scraps, licks plates.
Scales dog is seven times older than you think:
so he runs elliptically; so he cannot see spiders; so he is often distracted;
so he loses peanuts dropped at his feet; so he has suddenly become diabetic
and drinks from puddles; so there is bad wind in his system that came over
with the Mayflower; so he rolls on his back only once a week.
Scales dog is Gormenghast, is Nanny Slagg.
Scales dog is Horus, is Solomon Grundy.
His body makes disconnected music.
He is so old his eyes are glazed with blood;
so old wonders have ceased; so old all his diseases are benign; so old
he disappoints instantly; so old his aim is bad.

Scales dog is so old each day Scales urges him to die.
Scales dog puts on a show like a bad magician.
Scales dog squats as if he was signing the Declaration of Independence.
Scales dog is so old worms tired of him.
So old his fleas have won prizes for longevity.
So old his dreams are on microfilm in the Museum of Modern Art.
So old he looks accusingly.
So old he scratches for fun.
Scales dog was buried with the Pharaohs, with the Aztecs; draws social
security from fourteen countries; travels with his blanket; throws up on
the rug; has a galaxy named after him; Scales dog runs scared;
would have each day the same, the same;
twitches in his sleep,
wheezes.

In Brass and in Brimstone I Burn Like a Bell

Nearing the beast that baits:
Things close to the heart.
                              ('First
You remember the fox scattered russet
Before me, pelting down the Old Woman
So fast I had to keep running or else
Hit and stay put')

   Clammer of stones loud as blood;
   A moon more skin than shell
   To full eclipse.

Coming one with a shears and one with a bill-hook;
A boy with a glass of golden oil; chandler of hooks,
His nets hung like curtains; some wild and bewildered;
Some hawless, rank as a rake—

   'My hounds tore out my lady's life,
   But she stood bright upstanding'

—Phebus (for his brilliant hair) scorns
Those without malice on an easy *slauwe*,
Those drawing forfeit,

Backing off from real work like a horse
Backing off from a fire.

And the ringing of the game
As that which comes softly,
                              past hindrance,
By silent questing—

Swallows in a knot of air
Herring in a knot of water:
A great unravelling of silver fish
And silver birds

They would have love something other
That would have love whole.

2

The Shrug, the Hum, or Ha

Anoint the slug with salt or lye:
His appetite's a spattle trail
Before the slicks of mind and eye.

Tie fat on a limb for the sky:
So let it hang for jigget birds
Beyond the jinks of mind and eye.

Sparking spittle, fat and lye,
Slicks and jinks of mind and eye,
Spur, branch, and scauper's cry,
I light a start of calumny.

Princess Palestrina

At Princess Palestrina's he sat in an elevated *chaise* and
the fat lay on him in grey coils. He talked at length of the
writings of Nostradamus and, drawing a large quantity of snuff
into his nose, said it was his private opinion that he could
scarcely know men better than he did now, having studied them
closely, were he to live to fourscore. As for women he thought
it useless: they being so much more wicked and impenetrable.

When I assailed him for this disparagement to our sex (my face
as hot as my hands I am sure), he laughed in good humour and
asked if I understood the game of *tarrochi* which they were
about to play at. I answered in the negative, whereupon,
taking the pack from his boy, he desired to know if I had ever
seen such odd cards. I replied that they were very odd indeed.
He then fanning them said: 'There is everything in the world to
be found in these cards—the sun the moon the stars—and here,'
says he, throwing a card in my lap, 'is the Pope—here is the
Devil, and,' added he, 'there is but one of the trio wanting—
and him you may guess at.'

Undertow

As from the park's enclosure
    to eddy beneath the fall
Pair white and fair—plumes—
    wafted, circling in froth
Frounced, bucked by a wave-cockle
    tug to the clear fast run

   Have patience
              heart
   Have patience

Political Digression

I saw two go by
like dragon-flies
          joined

a kind of
      intercourse
from tail
to thorax—

the dry whisk
of eight beating
wings

Interrogations for the Justiciary

If there be any slaughter or murder.
If there be any fire-raising or burning.
If there be any ravishing of women.
If there be any theft.
If there be any reif.
If there be any reset of theft.
If there be any swindlers or night-walkers or sornars.
If there be any witchcraft or sorcery.
If there be any that slay red fish in forbidden time or their fry in milldams.
If there be any destroyers or peelers of green wood.
If there be any that maintain open trespassers.
If any person bring home poison and how they use it.
If any steal hawk or hound.
If there be any breakers of orchards or dovecots or gardens.
If there be any truce-breakers.
If there be any that steal other men's pikes out of their stands.
If there be any mutilation or dismembering of any person.
If there be any that sleep with other men's wives and destroy their good.
If there be any hoards found under the earth.
If there be any slayers of hares in the snow.
If there be any strikers of false money.
If there be any masterful beggars.

If any choose a task and abuse it.
If there be any interruption of rivers.
If there be any conjurers of air.
If any covet.
If any give false hire.
If any grow cold or wild against their neighbor.
If any beat down corn or lay waste.
If there be taint in calculation.
If any are bound to simplicity.
If any give pensions to the serpent in his path.
If any abjure.
If men build for strife or use only.
If there be women who accede.
If light is in any way scorned or disavowed.
If there is death in touch or breath.
If there be any desecration of grave-lots or lairs.
If any boat go unblessed.
If any star go unnamed.

Reticulum

'My daughter . . . O my daughter'

I
He was not a fat man
        but he gave the impression
of corpulence

something in his character
or presence
            let off the smell—
stale grease on a scullery shelf

And when he rose
it was to find the morning
grey and damp

a few crows
            hooting and grating
in a walnut tree by the driveway

II
'You fool   you *squid*
notorious
                jelly!'

        (popped his spouse
          and made him jump)

'Who stole *the cheese?*'

'Who stole *my silver comb?*'

                'That man
                    on the lawn
                who slew?'

'Goosed who   unloosed
Who double-seduced

Who *addled the brains of
Medousa*   our girl?'

III
Hands
     in the
     bathroom
mirror
     moved
     like veils
     before his
face

Quivering
     plastic
unsuspecting

he passed
  to an under
dimension
      of silt
and toothpaste
  and sluggish
propulsion

slipping
     almost
out of light
      in sea
and unilluminated
      mind

He was
    vaguely
aware of
        but never
discovered
            a morsel
of
    Stilton cheese
            ticking
in the pocket
        of his best
    flannel
pajamas

IV

'Daddy never new'
          (she wrote)
'what all I did for him'

'Daddy never gessed
          the trics I turned
          on the sligh'

'That creep outside   I coamed his throte
                   I stoned his one
                   good eye'

'Daddy never new'
          (she wrote)
'how careful it was plannd

                that spec of cheese
              his inky trail
          the reef where Mummy died'

'Daddy never new'
          (she sang)
'that I was on his side'

The Rumly Go

A birlin boat,
the shoggy ride,
the queerest scud
the wifie scryed.

'Mak up yer bed,
mak up yer mind,
a better loon
ye winna find.'

It's ever there,
and never slow,
but roon an roon
the rumly go.

Construct by Simple Succession

At the first stage there was a cellar
with beer bottles and carcasses
of various sorts

at ground level a reptile-house
and arboretum

the third was vacant/for let

the fourth had relics of the Virgin
some eye-teeth and finger-nail parings

the fifth had promises slick as an egg

the sixth entertained
a department of plumbing

the seventh a micklemoot

the eighth a crematorium

nine and ten an old printworks
        for Ascham's *Toxophilus*
in calf-bound quarto

eleven a baker-confectioner

twelve a group practice: one doctor
one dentist   one clergyman
one hypnotist

at the thirteenth floor something
you couldn't even hold out hope for

at the fourteenth glad blank attention

at the fifteenth tiled jordans

at the sixteenth pilgrims disgorged
by mistake and wandering down
passageways

at the seventeenth organpipes

at the eighteenth a bar called
The White Spotted Dog

Cassiopeia occupies the nineteenth floor
where the high jinks turn to snip-snap-snorum
and everything teaches be creature to fancy

the twentieth stage is sod roof and gargoyles
and the paraclete toasting his thoughts on
ripe temper

3

Lyke-Wake

ma s'averra ch'io mora
gridera poi per me la morte ancora

As an old man lags on the hillside, wagging
his stick where the sun burns over Caithness,
seeing the whole coast to Lossiemouth and beyond
the light on the rocks beyond the harbor mouth
the boats setting out for a night's fishing—
Lilt, Bezaleel, Glad Harvest—their nets drawn dry
from lofts and roadside fences, spread again to the sea

    light from eyes lighting to lids downcast
    light of table and firescreen   light of the last
    pewter candlestick

    earth's tapers trailing to rafter
    embers of face hand and wings

    Dawn has a grey list of cirrus and sky
    ma s'averra ch'io mora   if I have to die
    even death's mouth would kiss me
    even death's mouth would cry

    Now burned and buried
    lair-earth around you
    earth turned and dug under
    news let in a grey cirrus sky

light from eyes lighting to lids downcast
light of table and firescreen
this light to the drawstrings and spiked
pewter candlesticks
smoke of fine metalwork and carving

earth's tapers trailing to rafter
embers of face hand and wings

Let it draw in you   loose
curling in   let it breathe   sag of water
fly-bodkin bumping at walls and windows
let it speak in you   let it come through

lichen blank and lichen blazing
there as the day went by
stirring dust at her ankles
fish in distant pools

'in this wild a palace of green timber
bound with green birches both under
and above

and a queen to beggar description
wilderness robbed of its wind-drawn
distances

mirth and a perfect hunting
joined here since men took breath

in her eye
in one word to her people

floors laid with green scharets
and medwarts and flowers

grace of the founding line'

Dawn has a grey list of cirrus and sky
ma s'averra ch'io mora   if I have to die
even death's mouth would kiss me
even day's mouth would cry

and as dark draws in over Spey-fleets,
places of slaughter at the Bawds, at the Knock,
as men who never walked this break for near to thirty years
walk by Ruthven and Letterfourie, by the arches at Craigmin,
and gulls shadow high in off the water;
as burns go by hillslope and Lintmill barley in the sun's length,
cattle and all stir settle to sleep;
even as a child tries entrance to earth and air
tilth withers, wins: new yield plucked from the old

    Now burned and buried
    lair-earth around you
    earth turned and dug under
    watch let for a star-spread sky

4

Remorse

Idle eye
and gadding eye
    cry give give
like the horse-leech's
two daughters; no gain
as straight direction.

On the beach
a man gaffed
through throat
and head.

The thing
that bites
again.

Poem Beginning with Love as a Waterfall

Blithe
     thundering
looped over stone
     lipped
lenity

nothing prepares me for this

    turning
       like tellus
    turns
       obliquely
         to an engine
       of seasons

austerity   simple as water

    astonishing
       my grisly
    comforts

star-print and a gesture
  of virtuous refusal

the women were reapers
cutting low   level   and
clean

5

Link-Light

To see each man's existence traced out
   on a lintel   or a leaf   or sword
To see it there flaccid   scant
Or with the perfect substance   palpable
inscaped
Drawn to beauty like a single flower

To have a friend at your shoulder
To see the death of friends   and even
That death blazing that nothing would
extinguish
See the snake-rung map and pattern
Of which this is simply luminous part

There was a deer of the grey-ridge mountain
A people who heard the music of the rose-thorn
                   music of the night-bird
Who gave to a stranger the honor of hasard
A people sedulous in hunting and careful
To kill cleanly

This is their link-light
This is their blazing

The Dead-*Carn* Shifting Slowly in the Drift

Within limits of his competence which is love
Man makes a thing to demonstrate inheritance,
Assert the roots; draws stock from strength
As love draws breath from love's own kindling.

So in my mind-stem wakes this river
And mountains backing a coastal plain:
White Ash, the Bin, Ben Rinnes in calendar;
Wakes self, wakes county, established line,
Marked as the valid topography of mind
And changing matter, a judgement,
Whether larch-tassels crimson at shroving,
Whether dust at the door of an earth-house laid.
Wakes Badenoch the Wolf, skin webbed at his fingers;
Wakes fish from standing stones; wakes Culbin bells
Below marram and shore.

Flood cut open the bank;
Red clay and out-cropping sandstone
Curdled the silt-rust current,
Broke brimming in the firth
Like an opened vein.

Heraclitus pieced flow change and fire;
Heart and will at the river of desire.

A Slate Rubbed Smooth

Chronicle of the hunter of forms:
Of the white stag killed in the off-eye; grain struck
   dropped from the husk.
Given the distinction between what one does and what one is.
Between the world ignored and reckoned new;
Between perfect technique and perfect attunement;
Between this here now and everything else.

Willow and river-sand, rain-bangled water.
By Grantown fleet and Rothes to Fochabers' iron bridge
And bothies tar-streaked by Tugnet at the mouth
Sheer the Spey shifts.
Wind flattens grey-headed grasses,
Gulls lag or lapse to a sable sea.

Looking back to real beginnings, felicitous,
When the mind goes like a skipping stone across the water,
Planets at each dip, sun and simple air at every rise—
That man the master of hawks enjoyed his land free,
Had a hand-breadth of wax-candle to feed his birds
And light him to bed.

When he hunted, hawk and hunter shared the prey.

Traces

To see the first signs of the time: the seed-chap;
The way water travels beyond the reach of rivers and man.
Beginning with a thing converted; an equal mind in the face
    of blind contingency.
Beginning with the recognition of fact as a start for music.
Beginning with the eye and a sea-space.

Silver cars and copper—prows of silver and steel
Clap foam-flecks, heave bramble by stump.

Currents of scrub, great furrows of ebbing tide
Swivel to east, to pillars of woodland,

Jut of the pier-spiling rutted by spindrifts of light.

Nothing is inveterate: the direst habit of wind or
    circumstance wears new.
Even mockery or violent revenge—'That Roman in the Wall—
The stink of him—stewing from bracken, pile after pile.'
Beginning with bigotry and a degraded church;
A bone injured and decaying in the arm.
Beginning with gas, primordial, incandescent.
With a haggard hawk loosed from its traces.

It was to end with sea: a dark green swell,
Morning wind blowing gorse-smell and camomile
    to the ships brought round
To the anchorage of summer we had found—

Sloughed like a napkin one bird posts past reach
Coasts listlessly down by wave as you wade there
Something like sunlight, something like skin.

Riguarda

So let me set down
the wonder that begins
one glance from love
to love

how lightly we danced

a young girl gay
so grave and winsome

jeune pucelete
je sui sadete

joliete   plaisans

learning to please
myself and my sister

so let me set out
one step from love

So let me set out
one step from love

not distant
not curious

in thrall
to that or this

but liable
ardent

intending

careless of graces
we labor to be clear

So let me set down
the wonder around
the one loving laughter

a smile so winning
on the fairest face
of calm

stone light   ferry light
light off the water

at each place
my heart stops

to look at you

'In Fire the Voice Goes Further'

I
The thing we want
intuited; tongues
    precedent
    original

    tongues
    fountains

temper that sifts
and sorts what falls
between

    Things heedful
    augmented

direct
the infection
of feeling

II
The thing we want
    a shape
      cut
    in time

as a bird
    on the surface
    of the sea
snake-headed bird!

percept and concept
in lawful enactment
song-tangled

this to bless
    and this
for help

in fire the voice
goes further

song scapeless
external

III

The thing we want
      both riddance
      and memory

working
    by a kind
    of touch

and the look
when it comes
    full-fleshed

the rest consumed
like windlestraw

in gusts
of flame

7

At the Breaking of the Stag

At the breaking of the stag
bark stripped; the beast
unhided.

> Rump and pizzle
> and paunch and tail
> disbursed; the cods
> cut clean away.

> > Windpipe
> on a forked branch
> for presentation.

> Tripe and spleen
> and quartered heart.

> The *corbeles fee*
> cut last.

At the breaking of the stag
short shrift for surfeit.

Breaking through breast
and ribs and chine
> by fletches of fire

> a fine intent
> > against
> each quarry fallen

> the harried stag
> the doe transpierced

Here's a game played close
to the bone.

Of Akbar

I render the catalogue
of Akbar; of Iskandar's horse
washed in the fountain of life;
of Amber Head, his tasseled bridle;
of courtiers astounded by the lingam of ice;

further of a bauble—a bound man thrown
to dogs; of enclave; of ambit; of mustering
fancy; as demons pound chick-peas for tiffin
along the torrent side.

I give you the red woman
spinning before her tent; leopard
and lion silent at the tomb
of Bahram Gur.

I would set this down by
close particulars; each hummock
and fold of land; of trees the tamarisk
and grey-skinned sycamore; of birds
assembled the ring-dove and egret
and crested finch.

Laila languishes
and the stream runs clear; the pricket
tumbles to scent-spattered ground.

The Sooth of Birds

Hard dint to a good target;
a ring marked out for stones
at thirty paces

I'll sing at first for cunning
in the place where light
licks in

Chiming like the crab to take
some metal to my blood

and from stripped air devise
fresh weaponry

Sing for a ruse against close
pursuit   the sooth of birds
and all to fetch foison

Conjuring a land burst up by fire
                    and kelp-tangle
from the bottom of the sea

With shearwater gannet and shag
                    picked out
on a rock of that glittering
sea board

Skald
        of the
whipping wind

the *bitter* runes
whistled out

from his long-boned
bow

The Death of Odinn

Ominnis hegri heitir

The skerry stark, the sky
black-lead, the land's life
buckled hard in ice

nine days then hung
nine darks hung ganched
hung deadly down
the gallow's lord

horseman high in the thudding wind
the deep-tap tree a skittish ride

nine days nine darks
his own blind offering
wergild for the father fell

thirsting, fasting
hovering for wits of men
nine darks swept down
heart-stormed

howling at the root of light
rendering the deepest dark

more bitter than death
between his teeth
nine mighty songs
and the life to come

the skerry stark
the sky black-lead
landstream unfettered
weaving, sinuous

word flows on word like water
heart buoyant as a bird

and each thing done
built up from seed
            unfolds
to deep-tap tree.

Notes

Impresa An emblem or device; an undertaking.

In Brass and in Brimstone The Old Woman is a mountain by Broadford in Skye. The boy with a glass of golden oil derives from nothing I know directly—an image inserted at its own insistence. Hawless—have-less, destitute. There *was* a Gaston Phebus who wrote a treatise on venery and got his nickname for the reason given here. Malice—trickery, evasion. *Slauwe*— is like Tristan's *slâ*, a track or path or trail.

The Shrug, the Hum, or Ha Jigget and scauper are not neologisms, but not quite themselves either. Spattle and spittle are the same thing.

Princess Palestrina Whether the identity of this man might be determined in the country whose crown he claimed I don't know; I show him at a stage well removed from the figure of romance.

Undertow Two feathers dropped to the waterfall.

Interrogations for the Justiciary Reif—robbery, plundering. Sornars are spongers.

Reticulum Among other things, a netlike structure.

The Rumly Go Birlin—whirling; shoggy—shaky; scud—scud; scryed— descried in crystal or water; loon—lad; roon—round.

Lyke-wake Doctor Johnson defines as "the time or act of watching by the dead." The place names, like some in later poems, are close to the town where I was born.

Receipt Is also a station to await driven game.

Poem Beginning with Love Lenity—smoothness and lightness together; glissading. Tellus—I'm describing the earth's movement in relation to the sun.

Link-light Honor of hasard—a guest of the hunt might be placed in a position of risk—where they also had the chance to make first hit. Links or link-boys carried torches ahead of travelers at night.

The Dead-Carn The Wolf of Badenoch was Alexander Stewart, fourth son of Robert II of Scotland, who attempted to extend secular authority in the north. He and his "katerans" burned down Elgin Cathedral in 1390. If his fingers *were* joined by webs it would be unusual, but not altogether exceptional. The village of Culbin, situated at the mouth of the Findhorn—which is west of the Spey—was gradually inundated by sand. Marram is one of the binding sea-grasses.

A Slate Rubbed Smooth A bothy is a hut or lodging, here for salmon fishermen.

Traces Seed-chap—the first crack of the pod, as in broom or laburnum. This poem weaves in "Marine" by Rimbaud, as well as part of "Petit Air" by Mallarmé.

Riguarda Beatrice's words are: *"Riguarda qual son io."* The scraps of French are from an old anonymous motet.

In Fire the Voice Goes Further Windlestraw is chaff, bare grasses.

At the Breaking of the Stag The *corbeles fee*, like the corbin bone, was offered to carrion birds. Fletches are arrows or flights—as fletcher, an arrow-maker. Chine—part of the back, including the spine.

Of Akbar Pricket—a buck just showing nubs of horn.

The Sooth of Birds Foison is harvest, a force of life.

The Death of Odinn Skerry—a stretch of rocks; ganched—hung on hooks; wergild—a body price; landstream—a current in the sea from river waters. Tap—to liberate or extract; to open, break into, begin to use.